To Sloan, with love

Eve Bunting
THE BIG CHEESE

Illustrated by Sal Murdocca

M

ISBN 0 333 30071 8

First published 1977 in the USA by
Macmillan Publishing Co., Inc.
866 Third Avenue, New York, NY 10022
Collier Macmillan Canada, Ltd.

First published in Great Britain 1980 by
MACMILLAN CHILDREN'S BOOKS
A division of Macmillan Publishers Limited
4 Little Essex Street London WC2R 3LF
and Basingstoke
Associated Companies in Delhi, Dublin,
Hong Kong, Johannesburg, Lagos, Melbourne,
New York, Singapore and Tokyo

Printed in Hong Kong

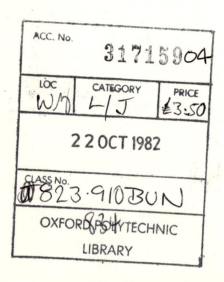

1

Miss Tillie Culpepper and Miss Bee Culpepper lived in a little old house at the top of a hill. There was a village with people at the bottom of the hill, but Miss Bee and Miss Tillie kept to themselves.

"Two's company, more's a crowd," Miss Tillie would say. "Never trouble trouble till trouble troubles you." And with that Miss Bee had to be content.

Every week Miss Tillie baked bread. They saved the crumbs that fell on their table, and every Sunday Miss Tillie made crumb ball for dinner.

"Waste not, want not," she always said, and Miss Bee would agree.

Sometimes Miss Bee thought it would be nice to go down into the village and buy something different to eat.

"In this house we save in season and spend with reason," Miss Tillie would say. "Enough is as good as a feast." And of course Miss Bee knew she was right.

One morning Miss Bee opened the front door and saw a big, round yellow cheese on the front step.

"Tillie," she called. "Come and see what someone has left on our front step."

"Hm," Miss Tillie said. "I remembered it bigger."

"You *knew* about it?" Miss Bee asked.

"Of course I did," Miss Tillie said. "I bought it."

"You never told me."

"Least said, soonest mended," Miss Tillie said. "Let's bring it inside."

It took both of them to roll the big cheese into their little old house.

"You bought it with money?" Miss Bee asked.

Miss Tillie sighed. "Ask a silly question and I'll give you a silly answer. Of course

You can never get too much of a good thing.

3

I bought it with money." Her eyes narrowed. "But not much money. A farmer's cart broke down. He had three of these and no way to get them to market. I told him to roll one up here."

Miss Bee blinked. "But there's so much!"

"A bargain's a bargain," Miss Tillie said. "And you can never get too much of a good thing."

They cut a piece of cheese to go with their bread for breakfast.

"This will last forever," Miss Bee said.

Miss Tillie agreed. "But there's something that's worrying me. There are some around who'd like to help us eat it."

"Who?" Miss Bee asked.

"Mice! We're going to have mice. And you know what they say about mice: 'A dirtier creature never was born. He'll gnaw on your vittles and nibble your corn.'"

Miss Bee nodded. They sat down in their rocking chairs to rock while they considered the problem.

"I know," Miss Tillie said at last. "We'll get a cat."

"A cat!" Miss Bee gave a little squeak of excitement.

Miss Tillie frowned. "Contain yourself, Bee. Remember what I've always told you: An empty vessel makes the most noise."

"Yes, Tillie. But, oh, a cat! A soft, furry cat to live with us. When will we get it?"

"Never put off till tomorrow what you can do today," said Miss Tillie. "Get your hat, Bee. We'll go right now."

2

Miss Tillie put all of their money in her black velvet purse. Together she and Miss Bee walked down the hill toward the village.

Miss Bee sniffed the air. "Oh, it's good to be going somewhere, Tillie," she said. "And I do declare! The honeysuckle is out. Spring is here already."

Miss Tillie sniffed too. "In the spring a mouse's fancy lightly turns to thoughts of cheese. We are not on a nature walk, Bee. Remember what I've always told you: Work before pleasure brings heavenly treasure."

"Yes indeed, Tillie," Miss Bee said. She tried to walk in a businesslike way along the main street of the village.

Halfway along the street they came to a

little shop with jars of fruit and trays of toffees in the window.

"Look, Tillie." Miss Bee pointed to a sign that was leaning against the glass.

The sign said CATS FOR SALE.

"Those that look are those that find," Miss Tillie said, and she pushed open the door.

A bell rang. Inside the shop were the good smells of ginger and molasses and ripe red apples. A fat lady stood behind the counter.

"Good day to you both," she said. "I'm Mrs. Wise."

"Good day to you," Miss Tillie said. "I understand you have cats for sale."

"I have indeed. Rabbits too, if you've a mind for one. Sugar for your tea and soap for your wash, oil for your lamps and potatoes for your pot. Whatever you need, I've got."

"A cat," Miss Tillie said firmly.

"Follow me," Mrs. Wise said.

7

Those that look are those that find.

A big gray tabby and her kittens lay in a basket in the corner of the kitchen.

"Just take your pick at a penny apiece," Mrs. Wise said. "And as good a buy as you'll ever find."

Miss Bee gave her little squeak of excitement. "Oh, Tillie," she said. "Just look at this one. He's got four white...."

Miss Tillie interrupted. "We don't want a kitten, we want a cat."

"In no time at all a kitten's a cat," Mrs. Wise said.

Miss Tillie frowned. "We need a cat that's a cat now. The mice are mice now."

"Ah, yes," said Mrs. Wise.

"Don't you think one of these kittens, Tillie...?" Miss Bee began.

"No," Miss Tillie said. "And hurry, Bee. We have to find a cat. Time and tide wait for no man, nor do mice. When the cat's away, the mice will play."

Mrs. Wise looked thoughtful. "There's a big tom cat who has been hanging around my backyard. I've asked, and no-body owns him. You could take him." She walked to the window. "There he is, on the wall."

Miss Bee and Miss Tillie looked out.

A sleek black cat with fur like satin sat on the red brick wall cleaning his whiskers. He stopped and looked straight at them. His eyes were as green as wet grass.

"Cat, Cat," Miss Bee crooned. She stood at the kitchen door.

The cat sat, unblinking. Then, with one spring, he leaped into Miss Bee's arms.

"Well, my lands," Mrs. Wise said. "I've never seen him take to a soul before."

Miss Bee carried the cat inside. "Look, Tillie," she whispered. "Isn't he beautiful!"

Miss Tillie sniffed. "Handsome is as handsome does." She opened her purse. "We'll take him."

"I'll have no money," Mrs. Wise said.

Miss Tillie snapped her purse shut.

A penny saved is a penny earned.

11

"We're obliged to you, Mrs. Wise. A penny saved is a penny earned."

The cat watched her from his clear green eyes. Miss Tillie glared back. "I hope you don't turn out to be worth what we paid for you," she said. "But I'm having doubts already."

"Shouldn't we at least buy something from her shop, Tillie?" Miss Bee whispered. "She's been so kind and...."

"Certainly not." Miss Tillie held her purse tightly under her arm. "It's more blessed to give than to receive, Bee. Haven't I told you that a million times?"

Mrs. Wise watched from her shop door as they walked together, the cat, Miss Bee and Miss Tillie, all the way back up the hill to their little old house at the very top.

That night, as they lay in bed, Cat purred like a well-oiled sewing machine. Miss Bee smiled in the darkness.

"Tillie," she whispered. "We're going to have such a life...the three of us."

Miss Tillie turned and her bed creaked. "Don't count your chickens before they're hatched," she murmured sleepily.

Miss Bee sat up. "Chickens! Little fluffy chickens with matchstick legs, chickens to love! We're going to get chickens?"

"No, we're not, Bee," said Miss Tillie. "A fool past forty's a fool forever. I'm afraid there's no hope left for you, Bee. Go to sleep."

❧ 3 ❧

"Now what will we do?" Miss Bee asked sadly. "We have to do something, Tillie. Just look at poor Cat!"

Miss Tillie examined Cat over her glasses. "He's all right. You can't judge a book by its cover."

"But he isn't a book, he's a cat, and he's hungry, Tillie."

Cat wasn't as sleek as when they'd first found him.

"He's not looking well at all," Miss Bee said. "We have to find something he can eat."

"Dumb Cat!" Miss Tillie said. "Don't you know that beggars can't be choosers? Why won't you eat my bread? Why won't you eat my crumb ball? Why won't you eat some of our big, round yellow cheese?"

14

You can lead a horse to water, but you cannot make him drink.

"Tillie," said Miss Bee. "That's what's wrong. Cats don't eat bread and cheese. And up here on the hill there's nothing for him to eat. He's scared away all the mice."

Miss Tillie broke off a crust of bread and held it under Cat's nose.

Cat turned his head away.

Miss Tillie sighed. "You can lead a horse to water, but you cannot make him drink."

Miss Bee nodded.

"Ah, well," murmured Miss Tillie. "To err is human, to forgive, divine." She sighed again. "We'd better make the best of a bad bargain. We need a cat to protect our cheese. We'll have to get a cow."

"A cow!" Miss Bee gave her little squeak of excitement and leaped up. "A warm, fat cow with big, soft eyes. A cow, bulging with milk for Cat. A cow to love. Oh, thank you, Tillie," she said. "When will we get the cow?"

Miss Tillie leaped up too. "The better

16

the day, the better the deed. We'll go right now."

Miss Tillie took her black velvet purse. Miss Bee tied a long string around Cat's neck, and together the three of them walked down the hill toward the village.

Miss Bee sniffed at the air. Cat stepped as lightly as a breeze.

"Oh, Tillie. It's so good to be going somewhere. Smell the blossoms. Look at the butterflies. Summer is here."

Miss Tillie marched on. "We'll need a good cow," she said. "You know what I've always told you, Bee. If a thing's worth doing, it's worth doing well."

"Indeed, Tillie, you have told me that."

They had almost reached the village when they met a farmer.

"Good morning, sir," Miss Tillie said. "We have come to buy a cow. Can you tell us where we might find one for sale?"

"I have a good cow myself," said the

17

It's not the quantity but the quality that makes the feast.

farmer. "She'll cost you fifty dollars and worth every penny."

"Does she give much milk?" Miss Bee asked timidly.

"Four buckets at night and four in the morning."

"It's not the quantity but the quality that makes the feast," Miss Tillie reminded him.

"Thick and creamy as hot-cake batter."

"Do you hear that, Cat?" Miss Bee whispered.

Cat swished his tail.

"Sold!" Miss Tillie opened her purse and took out fifty dollars. When she snapped the purse shut it had an empty sort of sound.

"Have we much left?" Miss Bee asked.

"Always taking out and never putting in soon comes to the bottom," Miss Tillie said.

The farmer pointed beyond a gate to where a fat white cow stood in the shade of a hawthorn hedge, chewing her cud. A small bell hung from a rope tied around her neck. "There she is, ma'am."

"She's as white as a snowdrop," Miss Bee whispered. She opened the gate and walked slowly toward the cow.

"Fools rush in where angels fear to tread," Miss Tillie muttered. "Don't hold out your arms, Bee. If that creature jumped into them, it would be the end of you."

"Pretty thing! Pretty Snowdrop!" said Miss Bee as she untied the rope and led the fat white cow back to the gate. "Isn't she beautiful, Tillie?"

"Beauty is only skin deep, Bee." Miss Tillie faced the farmer. "I hope she does what you say she does, but I've no way of knowing. The buyer needs a hundred eyes, the seller only one." She closed the gate carefully behind them. "We can go home now, Bee," she said. "An easy mind makes a light burden."

They walked together, the cat, the cow,

An easy mind makes a light burden.

21

Miss Bee and Miss Tillie, all the way up the hill to their little old house at the very top.

That night, as Miss Bee and Miss Tillie lay in bed, Cat purred and Snowdrop's bell jingled.

"Tillie," Miss Bee whispered. "We're going to have such a life...the four of us."

Miss Tillie turned and her bed creaked. "I just hope we haven't bought a pig in a poke," she grumbled.

Miss Bee sat up. "A pig! A pink, shiny pig with a curly corkscrew tail, a pig to love! We're going to get a pig, Tillie?"

"No, we are not." Miss Tillie sighed loudly. "They say that fortune favors fools, and for your sake, Bee, I hope so. Go to sleep."

4

"Now what will we do?" Miss Bee asked sadly. "Poor Snowdrop!"

Miss Tillie looked out of the window at the cow. Snowdrop's hide was gray and dull. Her head drooped. Her "moos" had a mournful sound.

"She's hungry." Miss Bee's voice shook. "We'll have to find something for her to eat."

Miss Tillie shook her fist at Snowdrop. "Dumb cow!" she said. "Why won't you eat my bread? Why won't you eat my crumb ball? Why won't you eat some of our big, round yellow cheese? Why won't you drink some of your own good milk?"

"Oh, Tillie," said Miss Bee. "Cows don't like bread and cheese and milk.

Cows eat grass, and there's no grass here on the hill."

Miss Tillie slammed the window shut. She sighed. "One bad thing leads to another. Life is only fuss and bother. I suppose there's nothing else to do. We need a cat to protect our cheese, and we need a cow to give milk for our cat. We'll just have to buy a meadow."

"A meadow!" Miss Bee gave a little squeak of excitement and leaped up. "A green meadow with white daisy stars and wild blue clover! When?" she breathed.

Miss Tillie leaped up too. "There's no time like the present, Bee. Get your hat."

Miss Tillie got her black velvet purse and took Snowdrop on her rope. Miss Bee put a long string around Cat's neck, and together the four of them walked down the hill toward the village.

Miss Bee sniffed the air. "Oh, Tillie, it's so good to be going somewhere. All of a sudden life is so exciting."

Cat purred, and poor Snowdrop's bell went ting, ting, ting.

"I hope this is the end of it," Miss Tillie said. "A rolling stone gathers no moss. It's time we settled down again."

On the way into the village they met the same farmer who had sold them Snowdrop.

"Good morning, sir," Miss Tillie said. "We need a meadow for our cow. A good meadow, a sweet meadow, a tried and true meadow. Do you happen to know of a meadow for sale?"

The farmer nodded. "I can sell you the very same meadow that was the cow's home. She'll take to it kindly, for she knows every nook and cranny of it."

"How much is it?" Miss Tillie pulled open the black velvet purse.

"Forty dollars."

Miss Tillie counted out forty dollars. Then she rolled up the black purse and put it in her pocket. "All good things must come to an end," she said. "And that's the end of that. A fool and his money are easily parted."

Snowdrop pulled on her rope. Her nostrils widened. She mooed happily. Then she went running through the long grass—stopping to bite the blossoms from a clump of clover and tossing her head so her little bell went ting, ting, ting.

Miss Bee looked around. "Is there anything in the whole world as beautiful as a meadow in summer?" she asked happily.

"Beauty is in the eye of the beholder," Miss Tillie said. "Don't ever forget that, Bee."

"I won't," Miss Bee said.

They sat in the white shade of the hawthorn hedge.

Miss Bee made a daisy chain for Cat's neck and a bigger one for Snowdrop's.

"This is the best day I ever had in my whole life," she said.

Miss Tillie got up and eased her bones.

Sitting is as cheap as standing.

"I do admit that sitting is as cheap as standing, Bee," she said. "But it's time to go home. Early to bed and early to rise makes us all healthy, wealthy and wise."

That night Miss Bee lay in bed with her arm around Cat, who purred loudly in the dark. On the porch, Snowdrop's bell trilled in the breeze.

"Isn't it strange," Miss Tillie said sleepily. "I don't think I would like it now if things were the way they used to be. You know what they always say, Bee. If you live with a goat you'll come to enjoy it."

Miss Bee sat up in bed. "A goat!" she said quickly. "A brown baby goat with little nubby horns, a goat to love! We're getting a goat?"

"No, we're not, Bee. You really are a sentimental fool sometimes." Miss Tillie yawned. "But then, if all fools wore white caps we'd look like a flock of geese. Go to sleep, Bee."

5

For a while everything seemed perfect. Each morning Miss Bee led Snowdrop down to Clover Meadow while Miss Tillie baked bread and churned butter. The big, round yellow cheese got a little smaller as the days passed. At night they slept to the music of Cat's satisfied purr and the gentle tinkle of Snowdrop's bell.

"I've never been so happy," Miss Bee said as she sat in her rocking chair one evening.

Miss Tillie stared glumly out of the window.

"Tillie?" Miss Bee's voice was anxious. "Something's wrong. What is it?"

Miss Tillie stopped rocking. "I'll tell you, Bee, for a trouble shared is a trouble halved, and you might be able to help.

After all, two heads are better than one."
She sighed. "You know what they say,
Bee. Too much, like too little, makes a
bad bedfellow."

Miss Bee waited.

"Milk," Miss Tillie said. "Butter."

Miss Bee looked around the kitchen.
There were seven buckets of Snowdrop's
milk. There were four buckets of thick
buttermilk and a panful souring for the
churn. There was enough butter on the
marble shelf for the whole town.

Miss Bee felt excitement rising inside
her. What kind of creature could they get
to eat the butter and drink the milk?

"Though I lived on a river, I'd not waste
water," Miss Tillie said.

Miss Bee nodded hopefully.

"I know!" Miss Tillie leaped out of her
chair. "There're more ways to skin a cat
than swinging it by the tail," she said.

Cat screeched and ran under Miss Bee's
bed.

There're more ways to skin a cat than swinging it by the tail.

"Not you, my love," Miss Bee crooned, getting down on her knees and peering under the bed. "Pay no mind to Tillie. That's just her way of talking."

"Get me the thick black pen from the button box," Miss Tillie said.

Miss Bee did, and Miss Tillie tore the bottom from a cardboard box and put it on the table. She chewed the end of the black pen and thought awhile. Then she printed in big letters:

FREE MILK

FREE BUTTER

APPLY WITHIN

She sat back and looked at the words with satisfaction.

"That ought to kill two birds with one stone," she said. "Now we'll wait and see which way the cat jumps."

"She's not talking about you, pet," Miss Bee told Cat.

The hungry eye sees far.

"We'll hang it out front this minute," Miss Tillie said. She fetched a hammer and three long nails.

"Now? But it's dark outside, Tillie. Shouldn't we wait until morning?"

"One today is worth two tomorrows," Miss Tillie said. "Haven't I told you that a million times?"

"But Tillie," Miss Bee said timidly. "Will anyone see the sign? They're down there and we're up here, all the way at the top of the hill."

"Never fear," Miss Tillie said. "The hungry eye sees far. We'll have callers. They'll know on which side their bread's buttered."

When they were cosily in bed, Miss Bee spoke. "You're so smart, Tillie. I just don't know how you think of these things."

"Necessity is the mother of invention," Miss Tillie said. "Go to sleep, Bee."

6

Early the next morning Miss Bee and Miss Tillie saw people coming up the hill. They were carrying buckets and plates.

Miss Tillie and Miss Bee slid pats of butter onto platters and poured milk into buckets.

"A friend in need is a friend indeed," Miss Tillie told everyone, and they all agreed.

All through the summer and into the fall the villagers came. They brought gifts of cabbages and apples, and eggs still warm from the hen.

"Fair exchange is no robbery," Miss Tillie would say, or "One good turn deserves another," and she would smile. Miss Tillie smiled more than she used to.

The hand that gives, gathers.

The shelves in the little old house creaked beneath the weight of all the food.

Guests came to share and sometimes stayed for supper, and the nights were warm with talk and laughter.

"The more the merrier," Miss Tillie told each new caller. "The hand that gives, gathers."

One evening, as they sat in their rockers before going to bed, Miss Bee said, "I declare, Tillie. There never was such a life. Having and sharing are the best things in the whole world."

Miss Tillie nodded. "A welcome friend adds seasoning to any meal," she said absently.

"And we have the nicest home," Miss Bee added.

"To every bird its nest is beautiful," Miss Tillie replied. But then she frowned. "You know, Bee, there are ups and downs in all things. The ladder of life is full of splinters."

"What's the matter, Tillie?" Miss Bee asked. "Do you want to tell me?"

Miss Tillie sighed. "Troubles never come singly, as the old woman said when her husband took sick and her hens wouldn't lay. Look around you, Bee."

Miss Bee looked all around the little old house. "What?" she asked.

Miss Tillie's face was stern. "There are none so blind as those who will not see." She pointed to a plate on which there was a small piece of cheese. "That's what's wrong."

"That?" Miss Bee peered at the cheese. "Why, it's almost finished, and we didn't waste a bit."

"Just so." Miss Tillie sat very still. "You can't eat your cake and have it too. When the cheese is gone, we won't need Cat to keep away the mice. If we don't have Cat, we won't need Snowdrop. If we don't have Snowdrop, we won't need Clover Meadow."

"Oh, no!" cried Miss Bee. "You don't mean we'll have to give them up? You love them too, Tillie."

Miss Tillie frowned and began rocking again. "I'm not denying it, Bee. What you never have you never miss, but I've had them now and I'd miss them. I guess I've been a bit of a fool myself, but he is not a wise man who cannot play the fool sometimes."

"I think you're *very* wise, Tillie," said Miss Bee softly.

"There's some that's wise and some that's otherwise," Miss Tillie replied. "When there's sense in the well it comes up in the bucket. You're never too old to learn, and when the heart speaks, the head should listen. I turned a deaf ear all these years, but I'm listening now, Bee. I'm making up for lost time."

Miss Bee nodded hopefully.

Miss Tillie sat forward. "Old habits die hard, though, and I'd listen easier if we could find a way to *need* Cat and Snowdrop and Clover Meadow. He who keeps what he doesn't need will need what he cannot keep. Even a bird should sing for his supper."

Miss Bee's eyes filled with tears. "Oh, Tillie," she wailed.

"Now, there's no use crying over spilt milk, Bee," said Miss Tillie. "Forewarned should be forearmed—but this time I'm not." Miss Tillie sat up straighter. "Heaven helps those who help themselves," she said firmly. "We have to put our noses to the grindstone, Bee. We have to think."

The moon rose in the sky. The stars came out one by one. Cat twitched. Snowdrop's bell chimed. And Miss Bee and Miss Tillie rocked the whole night through.

Toward morning Miss Tillie spoke. "It's always darkest before the dawn," she said. "Keep thinking, Bee."

The sky turned pink at the edges and then a startling gold.

Suddenly Miss Tillie leaped out of her chair. "I've got it, Bee. It's a long road that has no turning. I see the light at the end of the tunnel."

Miss Bee tottered up. "What, Tillie? What?"

"Don't keep me back, Bee. I've work to do."

"Work? *Now*?"

"Of course, now. It's now or never. The

sleeping fox catches no hens. Out of my way, Bee."

Miss Tillie tied her apron strings and rolled up her sleeves. She scalded the churn and poured a bucket of sweet milk into it. Then she began plunging the paddle up and down, up and down, faster and faster.

"What are you doing, Tillie?" Miss Bee asked timidly.

"I'm saving the day. I'm pulling the chestnuts out of the fire. I'm taking the bull by the horns, Bee."

"Are you making more butter, Tillie? Can I help?"

"Thank you, no. Too many cooks spoil the broth...or the cheese."

"You're making *cheese*? But, Tillie, I can't bear the thought of one more crumb of cheese. I can't bear the thought of even the *smell* of cheese!"

Miss Tillie's face was red. "Sometimes the cure seems worse than the disease, Bee.

Where there's a will there's a way.

But we have to choose the lesser of two evils. What can't be cured must be endured. In this life, Bee, we have to take the good with the bad, the rough with the smooth. He who wants eggs must listen to noisy hens." She stopped for breath. "There's no accounting for tastes. Our new friends like cheese, and there's nothing lost that a friend gets. We'll make it, they'll take it. The *smell* will bring the mice, so we *will* need Cat. The longest journey starts with a single step, Bee. The place to begin is at the beginning."

Miss Bee clapped her hands. "Oh, Tillie, you're wonderful!"

Miss Tillie smiled. "You see, Bee," she said, "where there's a will there's a way, and all's well that ends well. Man does not live by bread alone, Bee. Haven't I told you that a million times?"

"Yes, Tillie, oh, yes indeed!"